Neria

by David Corke

with the assistance of
Leo Braithwaite
Mattia Curtotti
Kalevi Harkonen
Noah Hirst
Ashton Hughes

The five boys (aged 8-9) who helped write this book are members of the Walden Countryside Wild Child Club.

All royalties from this book will help fund the Club.

Search: Walden Countryside Wild Child

www.walden-countryside.co.uk

First published 2021

ISBN 978-19164631-3-4

Foreword (for Mums & Dads)

This story has been created by and for a "Wild Child" group of home-educated youngsters who, during the lockdown period of the Covid 19 pandemic when restrictions kept everyone at home, met only by Zoom. Each week we read a new chapter, talked about it and suggested what might happen in next week's session. When we started no one knew how the story would end and, as you will find, we are still not certain.

The story line concerns a boy from our own (locked down) time and a girl from the Stone Age. They explore each other's worlds. To the girl, our world is full of magic and magicians who can light matches, switch on electric lights and tame wild animals. To the boy, the Stone Age is an exciting but strange place where he finds the girl knows much more about nature and how to survive than he does.

I hope the fairly short chapters will make it suitable as a book to read to children or for those who have recently learnt to read.

The book is intended to do a little teaching, within a story that I hope children will enjoy. The Wild Child group certainly enjoyed helping to create it.

The little "Things to think about" sections at the end of each chapter are optional - but again the Wild Child Club members enjoyed discussing some of these points.

CONTENTS

Chapter 1 The Hot Springs

I live miles from anywhere, at the end of a long forest track leading to the valley where our farm is. It takes nearly an hour to get from my home to school but now the schools are all closed for the summer and I only see my school friends on Zoom. The rest of the time I'm a farmer. Dad says that in the olden days someone who was ten would be out working on the farm all day and I had better get used to living in the olden days now I'm not at school.

Most days my work is just to climb up the path towards the mountains and check that all our sheep are OK and still in the fields where they are supposed to be. There's never been any problem with the sheep and so I have plenty of time to enjoy myself alone in the hills and what I enjoy most is swimming in the hot springs.

There's a little stream that runs down the valley from our sheep fields and even in winter the water is quite warm near where it bubbles up at the base of a cliff. It runs into a big pond before starting off down our stream on its way to the river. The pond is like an outdoor warm swimming pool and we try to keep it a secret, so that lots of tourists don't find it. But now there aren't any tourists anyway.

Today, like most days when I have finished checking the sheep, I took off my clothes and had a lovely swim. Then I lay in the sun to get dry.

Suddenly, before I was ready to get dressed again, a girl appeared from behind a bush: she must have been hiding in the entrance of the cave that is just next to where the hot spring bubbles up. She had undressed too, so I expected she wanted to swim too. She looked at me, smiled, and said something but I couldn't understand a word of what she said.

I can only speak French but the people on the other side of the mountain speak Spanish. I can't speak Spanish but I know what it sounds like and some words sound the same as French. It wasn't Spanish she was speaking. Mum and Dad had told me that, further along the mountains, towards the Atlantic Ocean, people speak a language called Basque that is different from all other languages. Maybe she was speaking Basque.

Even though neither of us could understand the other, we started to try. She pointed to herself and said "Neria" and then pointed at me. I pointed at myself and said "Édouard". So then we knew each other's names. Then it turned into a game - we took turns to point at a bit of each other and saying the name, which the other would then say in their own language. I soon knew the words for head, nose, ears, arm, leg, foot, willy, belly button and quite a lot more.

Then we had a swim. "Swimming" I said and Neria's reply taught me another word. Next we started doing things we could describe: stand-up, sit-down, run, walk and so on.

When it was nearly tea-time, and I needed to go home, we had just started to be able to understand each other's language a bit. She signalled by putting her head on one side, resting it on her hands and closing her eyes. Either she was tired or she was saying she wanted to go home or maybe she was asking where I would go to sleep. I pointed to my house way off down the valley and signed that I eat my food and sleep there. She pointed into the cave and made the same signs.

I got my clothes and started to get dressed. Neria went into the cave and came out again with her clothes. They were really weird: some pants and a vest made of fur and, on top, some floppy trousers and a kind of pull-over jerkin with an animal design on the front, both made with animal skins that were still a bit hairy. Her boots were made from thicker leather without fur. I thought her clothes were rather ugly.

Neria was making a last attempt at language learning – she pointed at the sun and I told her its name. Then she said "sun" in her language and pointed to show it going right across the sky to set in the west, then rising again in the east. I made the sun-setting sign. Then the going-to-sleep sign. Then the sun-rising sign. Then she pointed at her self and me.

I said "Neria and Édouard?" and she said the same and disappeared into her cave.

I think she means we can meet tomorrow. I'm already looking forward to seeing her again but I don't think I'll tell Mum and Dad about her yet. They would only think I was making up stories.

Things to think about

- Do you think Édouard is imagining Neria or is she real?
- If she is real, where might she live?
- Why does she wear funny clothes?
- If you met someone who couldn't speak your language, how could you learn to talk with them?
- What will Édouard and Neria do tomorrow?

Chapter 2 Cow's Milk and Reindeer meat

The next day Dad asked me to help with the cows in the morning. At that time the cows that we milked each day shared a field with those that had stopped giving milk and with the heifers that were too young to have calves yet. We needed to separate them so the bull could be put with the cows that had stopped giving milk and the heifers needed to stay out of the bull's way until they were old enough to get pregnant.

It didn't take long to finish the task and Dad asked if I'd walk the three heifers up to the sheep fields and let them live with the sheep for the rest of the summer.

"You can take some food with you and have a swim afterwards" he added.

I took my lunch sandwiches and headed for the hills. It's not difficult walking heifers – you put a rope round the neck of the friendliest one and lead it like a dog, the other two just follow.

There was no problem with the sheep and they seemed quite happy to share their field with the young cows. It was time for a swim and, I hoped, to meet Neria.

She stepped out from the entrance to the cave just as I arrived. I think she must have been watching me for some time. She seemed fascinated by the sheep and the cows and obviously had loads of questions she wanted to ask but she didn't know enough French.

I'd brought my lunch-time cheese sandwiches with me, so when she got out a little leather bag with some food in it we sat beside each other for a picnic. I looked at what she was eating: some cooked meat and a kind of vegetable paste with green leaves and stems mixed with stuff that looked like brown mashed potato. I wanted to know what it was and pointed at it and tried to ask. She thought I wanted to try it and gave me some meat and vegetable mix. It really tasted very good so I offered her some of my bread and cheese sandwiches and a bite of my apple. She obviously thought I had good food too – but what was hers?

I pointed at her meat and then at the cows and said "moo" and she said no. So I pointed at the sheep and said "baa" and she said no again. Then she got down on hands and knees, pretending to be an animal, then used her hands spread out and held up beside her ears. She was being a deer with antlers. So that was what the meat was. So I taught her the word for a roe deer in French (that's the smallest of our deer) and she told me what deer were called in her language: it sounded like "elur-oreinak". I wondered what sort it was and used signs to ask if it was a big or small deer. She signed back and said it was really big – then she did some more signing. She pretended to be a mother holding a baby so it could drink its mother's milk. Then she did the antler signs again. At last I realised what she meant: the mother deer had antlers like the male ones. So elur-oreinak must be reindeer because it's only reindeer where the females have antlers. Where do reindeer live around here? I'd never seen one, not even on Christmas Eve.

I wanted to know what her vegetables were but it was her turn to ask the questions. What was my cheese? I tried to say it was made from cow's milk: I pointed at the cows and told her how to say cow. Then I pointed at their udders and mimed milking a cow. She looked puzzled for a bit, then she realised and pointed at her own chest and pretended to let a baby suckle again. She said her word for milk and I said yes.

Explaining about bread was even more difficult than cheese: there weren't any fields of wheat this high up, so I picked some grass with seed heads and signed how you could get seeds from big grasses and grind them up and then mix them with water and cook them to make bread.

It was easier for her to tell me about her vegetables. She picked some young stinging nettles then she pulled up some plants with feathery leaves whose roots looked like brownish, thin carrots. So her lunch was boiled nettles and mashed up wild carrots. It tasted jolly good. Why can't you buy tins of reindeer, nettle and wild carrot in the supermarket?

I tried to ask her where reindeer lived round here. and she took me into the cave . There, right at the back, where there was just enough light to see it, was a painting of a reindeer. I couldn't understand what Neria was saying about it though.

It was time to go home but we both made it clear we would meet again tomorrow. This time it wasn't all signs. We knew how to say something like "see you tomorrow" and she kissed me goodbye.

I'm looking forward to tomorrow.

Things to think about

- What was your last meal? What was in it? What was it when it was still a living plant or animal?
- Where do people who still eat reindeer live?
- What might Neria bring to eat tomorrow?

Chapter 3 A Mammoth Feast?

Dad had no work for me next morning so I asked to go up to the sheep with my lunch and stay there afterwards to see if I could spot any eagles or vultures. I didn't say anything about Neria - she was my special secret. I was certain she'd be there again today and she was.

We were going to have lunch together and learn some more words. My sandwiches had sardines in them and she saw they were fish straight away. I didn't know if her word meant any sort of "fish" or only "sardine".

She had meat again but it was different from yesterday's reindeer - for a start it was still raw. It was a big lump of meat dripping with red blood. Surely she wasn't going to eat it raw? No, she was going to cook us both a meal and she started gathering sticks and arranging them on top of some dry grass that should be easy to light. Neria went back into the cave and carried out a big stick that had been alight and was still glowing at one end. She blew on it, trying to get it properly alight so she could start the fire. It went out and she said a short word very loudly. I didn't need to ask her what the word meant. Fortunately, I had a box of matches in my pocket so I got one out, struck it and lit the fire. She looked absolutely amazed and kept saying "Magia".

When the fire was going properly we picked a bunch of nice young nettles and stuffed them into holes she made in the lump of meat. Then she covered the meat up with ashes at the bottom of the fire. While the meat cooked we had plenty of time to ask each other questions. I asked her what "magia" meant and she said she would show me. She collected five little round pebbles and gripped them in one hand. Then she threw them, all at the same time, and caught them in the other hand. Then she opened one hand and showed it was empty and so was the other when she opened that. She reached across and retrieved one of the pebbles from behind my ear and did the same four more times until she had all five pebbles in her hand. Then she threw them away. So she thought striking a match was a conjuring trick and I suddenly realised that we had found a word that was nearly the same in French and in Neria's language. "Magia" is the same as "Magie".

I got my match box out again and got a match out slowly and showed her which end was going to catch fire. Then I struck it and she squeaked with surprise and seemed to have no idea how I had done my magic trick. But then I didn't know how she had done hers.

I thought I'd show her some real magic: I got out my phone and took a picture of her. I showed her the picture and she was absolutely amazed. So I showed her which buttons to press and she took a picture of me.

I pointed at the cooking meat and said "deer?" She said no and signed to say it was a really big animal and then leaned forward and held one arm so it looked as though it were attached to her head and waved it to and fro like the trunk of an elephant at the zoo. Then she made a trumpeting sound just like an elephant. Her name for the animal was "mamutxoa" – quite like those elephants we call "mammouts" in French. She was saying she was cooking me a chunk of mammoth meat. But mammoths have been extinct for thousands of years. She might be good at magic tricks but not that good.

I asked her where the mammoths lived and she said she would show me when I could speak her language a bit better.

She added "You can get there on a path through the cave".

It was a really good meal and afterwards we had a swim and washed all the mammoth grease off our hands and faces. When we were dry and dressed she kissed me goodbye and said:

"See you tomorrow" and I replied:

"And some mammoths soon I hope" just as she disappeared.

When I got home it was only an hour to our evening meal. I wasn't very hungry and sat thinking about Neria and what might happen tomorrow.

Mum said "What's wrong Édouard? You haven't eaten much and you look as though you are worried about something."

I replied "No I'm fine Mum, it's just that I'm not feeling very hungry. I had a mammoth meal at lunch time."

Things to think about

- When did mammoths live in our world?
- How do matches work?
- What ways might Neria's family be able to start fires without matches?
- What other animals might live in Neria's world?

Chapter 4 The Mammoth Hunt

I was determined to learn Neria's language and get taken to see the mammoths and she was just as keen to learn French from me. We met every day for a fortnight and practised very hard. She was really good at knowing the names of all the plants and animals that we saw. Often I didn't know a plant's name in French so I just used her word for it.

Everyday Neria was waiting for me near the hot spring. She was never late and, one day, I asked her how long she had to wait.

"It used to be a whole day" she replied and then explained why.

"When I go home it is always exactly the same time as when left – so no one ever notices that I've been missing. The only problem is, if I've spent a long time with you, I'm quite tired when I get home and there's still loads of work waiting to be done. So I usually have a sleep in the cave before I go home.

The real problem is that the same thing happens when I come through the cave to you: it is the same time here as when I had left you and I have to wait right through the night before you come back. If I have a good long sleep in the entrance to the cave then it is early morning when I get here I only have a few hours to wait for you."

In one way this was really good news: if the cave worked the same way for me, I would be able to go and see the mammoths in Neria's world and then get home without anyone knowing I'd been away.

At last she said we were ready for a visit to her world.

"Come early tomorrow."

Before I went to bed that night I Googled "Mammoth" and learned quite a lot about them. They are certainly extinct, and I hope Neria isn't just joking. Well, it will be fun to find out tomorrow.

Neria was waiting for me at the hot spring all fully dressed in her rather ugly leather clothes. She had another set of clothes with her and said I should leave all my clothes at the cave entrance and put on her spare set, so I would look like someone from where she lived. She said her people wouldn't believe her if she said I came from a world a where animals were tame and I could make fire with little magic sticks.

When she had shown me how everything fitted, and had helped me lace-up my boots, she led me into the cave. She had a smouldering stick that she blew on and got it burning properly at one end, where a lump of fat was tied on.

She held the other end of the torch aloft, so we could see where we were going. I'd explored the cave before but never found the tiny little tunnel whose entrance was hidden behind a rock. At first the tunnel was dark but then I saw daylight a long way in front of us. When we stepped out of the tunnel we were in a different world: Neria's world.

Neria signalled me to follow her: "We don't want to be seen by everyone and get told to do some work."

Nearly everywhere was open grassy countryside with just scattered trees and bushes. The really exciting things were the animals: there were lots of wild horses and bison (I'd only ever seen bison in the zoo or on television before). What I could see seemed a bit like the television films of Africa except the herds of African zebra were horses and the wildebeest were bison. And it was really quite cold, not hot like everyone says Africa is.

Neria pointed into the distance and said:

"There's usually some mammoths in the long reeds down by that big river" and we set off across the grassy plain to find them.

The horses and bison ran away whenever we got anywhere near them.

When we got near the river we could see wide paths going into the reed beds and we could hear the mammoths trumpeting sometimes. We crept along one of the paths until we could see four mammoths pulling up great bunches of reeds with their trunks. One of them was a baby.

Neria whispered "We'd better go back before they see us. Mother mammoths get really fierce if they think you might hurt their baby".

When we were a safe distance away, we sat down on some rocks where we could watch the horses and bison and eat the lunch Neria had brought. It was pieces of cooked meat that we ate with lots of the bilberries that were growing all round us. There weren't any springs or streams near us but Neria had a leather bag with her that was full of water so we shared that.

Then I needed a wee, I found a bush but I couldn't find the right opening in my leather trousers. I think they were made for a girl and I had to lower them like girls do.

I tried to work out where we were: unless going through the cave had taken us to a completely different world it must have taken us back in time to when mammoths were still around and people lived in caves. The sun and all the animals and plants, and Neria of course, all looked like things we knew in my world so I decided it was our world but we must have gone back in time. How long ago was that?

I couldn't think of the words to ask Neria what the date was. It wouldn't have made any sense to her anyway: we say the date is how many years since Jesus was born. Well he hadn't been born when there were mammoths and it seemed unlikely Neria would know how long she would have to wait for the first Christmas.

We started walking back to the cave and on the way we met a couple of grown-ups. The man carried a spear and the woman a dead mountain hare. Neria obviously knew them and I heard her say my name so she must be telling them where I came from. When they were gone I asked if she had told them about my world.

"No, they wouldn't have believed me, so I said you were a dream-time friend."

I was puzzled:

"Can other people see your dream-time friends?"

"Of course they can, at least sometimes, just like people can sometimes see the dryads that live inside the trees or the spirits of the animals."

Well, everything was different in her world so I suppose it makes sense here.

It had been hours since we first arrived in mammoth country and there was a long part of the path left to reach the cave and my home. I found the right words to tell Neria I had to go home because it was late.

She said "I've explained that lots of times - when I get home from visiting your world, it is exactly the same time I left."

She was certain it would work the same way for me and that I would find it just the same time when I got home as when I left.

I didn't quite believe her but she said it always worked that way for her when she visited my world.

"Anyway I'll come with you and you can show me something of your world. But we shouldn't go yet: it will be early morning in your world and it is evening here. We should sleep here and then go to your world"

So we made a bed of dry grass in the entrance to the cave and curled up together until morning.

She said I could keep my leather clothes and hide them in the cave where my own clothes were. We went through the cave and it was morning in my world too.

I put my own clothes back on then I realised we had plenty of time for a swim before I went home so I started to take my clothes off again.

As I was getting ready for our swim I thought about Neria's world. If I had stayed there for ten years would it have still been today when I got home? And would I still be ten, or twenty? Would I like living in Neria's world?

But the real problem was how can I show her my world? What will Mum and Dad say?

Things to think about

- Where did the very first humans live? Was it like Neria's country?
- Fairies are sort of "dream-time friends" that we only have in stories now, Once people really believed they could see them. What other sorts of imaginary beings did people once think were real?
- Édouard wondered what would happen if he stayed ten years in Neria's world then got back to his world. Would he be a ten-year-old boy again or a young man of twenty? What do you think?
- If Édouard takes Neria to meet his Mum and Dad, what will they believe about where she comes from?

Chapter 5 Milking Cows and Meeting Parents

Neria was already swimming in the warm lake, so when I had finished undressing I dived in too. We had a couple of swimming races and she won both of them, so I was quite glad when she wanted a rest from swimming.

We flopped down on a big flat rock that had been nicely warmed by the sun and waited for us both to get dry. She asked about the heifers that I had put in with the sheep some time ago. She pointed at them and said "behiak" and at other times "behia" so I asked what the difference was. She held up one finger and said "behia" then three fingers (because there were three cows) and said "behiak". In French the word for one cow sounds just the same as for three cows.

Then she wanted to know where the "zezena" was. I was puzzled until she pointed at herself and said "cow" and then at me and said "zezena" so I decided that what she meant was "boy cow" and I could tell her that our word was "bull".

It was quite difficult to explain that the bull was with the grown-up cows near the farm and these were young cows that hadn't had calves yet (her word for calves was txahalak).

So I'm still learning her language even though I thought I was doing quite well at it days ago.

She wanted to see the other cows and find out how we got milk from them.

"How do you get them so tame? Our cows are wild and run away when you get near or attack you if you get to close to their calves – just like the mammoths and all our other wild animals."

I explained that our cows had all been born in our fields, as had their mothers and grandmothers, so they knew people weren't dangerous and that we would make sure they always had plenty to eat.

"Why do they let you take their milk – don't they want it for their calves to drink?"

I explained that the calves did drink their mother's milk at first but then we took the calves away and milked the cows for ourselves. A cow goes on making milk for ages if you keep on milking it.

Neria wanted to see the cows being milked and that would mean taking her to our farm and letting her meet my Mum and Dad. Should I go and get some of my clothes for her, so I could pretend she was someone from my world? That is what she had done when she took me to see the mammoths.

I decided it would be better to tell the truth and see if I could get my parents to believe me. It wouldn't be easy though.

As soon as I got near the house Mum and Dad came out and asked me:

"Who's your friend? You know you are not supposed to play with other children except at school.".

The only thing I could think to say was:

"She was up the hill where the sheep are, I don't think her home is near here because she doesn't speak French - except what I've taught her. She's called Neria."

Mum asked Neria the name of her house. She didn't understand.

"Do you know your telephone number?" She asked what a telephone was. Mum asked what her Dad did:

"Hunting mostly, he's good at killing bison."

Mum was obviously getting worried. Were these two kids playing some sort of game? I usually told the truth and she could easily tell when I was making things up. Whoever she was, Neria seemed to be lost and a long way from home. Her parents must be really worried about her. So Mum telephoned the police station and explained about having found a lost child. They wanted to know all about her and said no one had reported a missing girl. Please would Mum take a photo and email it to them, so they could get police all over France to see if they recognised her?

Someone who works for the council, taking care of children who need taking care of, phoned up. She said that normally the council would look after a lost child until she could go home but it was difficult now because of the rules about not letting children mix with other children from different families. Would we look after Neria until they had found her parents? Of course Mum and Dad said yes.

Mum thought Neria's clothes could do with a wash, or cleaning somehow, and went to find a set of my clothes that would suit her. I haven't got a sister, so she had to wear boy's clothes but jeans, tee-shirt and pullover do just as well for girls as boys.

The cows had already been milked, so Dad told Neria she could help milk them tomorrow morning. It was time for dinner.

After dinner it was getting dark so Dad switched on some lights. Neria cried "Magic" and wanted to know how you could get light just like that, without having to light a fire.

Dad just said "It's electric, when you switch it on the electricity makes the light–bulb glow brightly."

I could see that Neria didn't understand at all: how could I explain electricity to her? Could I even explain it to me?

It was almost bedtime and Mum got a bed ready for Neria in our spare bedroom and gave her some of my pyjamas and a new tooth brush.

I had to show her how to brush her teeth. She whispered to me that she needed to go outside for a wee and so I had to show her the toilet next to the bathroom and explain how girls need to sit on it for a wee not just for a poo.

Then Mum took her to her bed, persuaded her to put on her pyjamas, got her into bed and kissed her good night. Neria started crying loudly.

"People never have to sleep on their own. Why do I have to have special sleeping clothes – I always keep my ordinary clothes on and sleep with all the other children and grown-ups round our big fire."

Mum relented a bit and asked if she would like to share a room with me: I've got a spare bed in my room.

As soon as Mum and Dad had tucked us up and gone downstairs, Neria came and climbed into my bed. We snuggled up and woke just in time for breakfast and the morning milking.

At that time we had only got six cows that gave milk and we milked them all by hand. Dad says it is better that way because cows don't like milking machines and the cheese tastes better when they are hand-milked.

It didn't take long to show Neria how it was done and after a couple of attempts she could get the milk to squirt into the bucket just as well as I could.

I asked if I could go and check the sheep like I usually do and could Neria come too? Mum was still worried about where Neria's home was, and when the police or council lady would come and take her home, but I promised we would come straight back. I put some extra clothes on and Neria wanted to get back into her own skin clothes.

As we walked up towards the sheep fields Neria said "I want to go home and see my Mum and Dad. You can come too."

I said that I'd promised to go home straight away and to get her back safely with me.

Neria was certain we could visit her parents and be back at my house before the evening meal.

"You know how the cave tunnel works: when I go back from your world to mine I always get home at the same time as when I left. It's the same for you – when we saw the mammoths you got home at the same time we had left here. If we go together, we'll get to my home when I left yesterday and when we come back it will still be today and we can get home to your parents really quickly. It won't matter how long we stay in my world.

It sounded a great plan: it should be really exciting, perhaps I could go hunting with her Dad – I just hoped it would work. I put on the skin clothes that Neria had given me for my first visit to her world.

What will we see this time?

Things to think about

- Neria lives in a world where all the animals are wild and there is no electricity. What other things in Édouard's world would seem new (or magic) to her?

- If you met someone from another world and took them home with you, what do you think your Mum and Dad would say?

- If you were visiting someone else's family would you mind sleeping in a room all on your own? Would you mind if everybody slept in the same room? Or around a camp fire?

Chapter 6 Feeding Babies

We arrived at the cave entrance and even though it was a nice day we didn't want to waste time having a swim.

Neria hadn't got a flame torch, and I didn't have an ordinary torch, so we went through the cave by feeling our way along the walls until we could see Neria's world at the end of the tunnel.

We went straight to Neria's home which was in the entrance to a huge cave with a big fire burning at the mouth of the cave. No one seemed very surprised to see me and Neria didn't need to pretend I was her dream-time friend. She just said I lived a long way away and she had met me when she was out on her own.

She asked "Can he stay here with me for a while?"

Everyone seemed to think it wasn't unusual for a boy to wander off from home and go to stay with other families.

Some men arrived with a dead bison calf tied to a pole which it took two men to carry. Neria said "Hello Dad" to one of them. They were busy cutting the bison's skin off and didn't seem likely to invite me to go hunting with them today. Neria said that our job for the afternoon was to look after the baby kids. Not the really new babies, each Mum wore her baby in a kind of pouch on her front – the Mum could usually let the baby drink her milk while the baby was in its pouch.

All four of "our" babies were crawling about or just starting to walk and were learning how to eat proper food and it was our job to feed them. Neria went to the fire and got some bones with cooked meat on them. She bit off a big lump of meat and started chewing it and I said:

"I thought we were feeding the babies not you."

When she had chewed the meat into a mush she picked up a baby, stuck out her tongue with mushed meat on it and let the baby eat it. Then she fed another baby the same way.

She said "We call it kiss-feeding. I like doing it, do you want to try?"

I didn't really want to but I thought I ought to say "yes". It wasn't horrid at all, it was quite fun having a kid grinning up at you and being so pleased when you fed it. The babies didn't have nappies so, when they were all fed, we had to use quite a lot of the dry moss that was by the fire, to clean them up. That wasn't so nice as feeding them.

Neria said we must get more moss to dry for next time and we had to walk a long way to a big, marshy pond that had lots of moss growing round the edge. It was the sort of moss that is like a sponge: if you squeeze it lots of water runs out, then it dries beautifully by the fire.

There were some other children hunting round the edge of the pond and I asked Neria what they were looking for.

"Frogs, it's the children's turn to catch dinner tonight."

"Surely you don't eat frogs?"

"Why not, you eat fish and frogs are just fish with legs. They taste good too."

When they were dead the frogs went in a big clay pot: it looked a bit like the clay that some flower-pots are made from. Then Neria's Mum and the other mums added lots of roots and leaves of different plants and the pot was left in the ashes at the edge of the fire, until the frog stew was ready. I tried not to think about the frogs and pretended they were fish as I ate them. Frog fish are really good. Afterwards we helped ourselves from a big basket of raspberries. The hunters had brought them home: Neria said raspberries didn't grow very near to where we were.

It was getting dark when we had finished the meal and everyone started to get ready for bed, even the grown-ups. I suppose that, when it gets dark and you haven't got electricity, there's not much else to do.

One of the men told a story: it didn't seem to be a bedtime story just for children. Everyone listened to it but he used complicated words and I couldn't really understand what it was about.

Everyone kept their daytime clothes on and a pile of soft skins were spread round the fire, to be used like blankets. Neria and I snuggled up together, like she had wanted to when we were in my bedroom. We had almost gone to sleep when there was a flash of lightning and clap of thunder. I cuddled Neria a bit tighter just in case she was frightened, then she cuddled me too in case I was afraid. There was only the one clap of thunder and we soon got to sleep afterwards. Then it was morning and everyone got up at first light.

Before this adventure with Neria had started I hadn't thought much about what it would be like to be a caveman (or a cave boy). Cartoons had men in silly clothes running around killing animals with bows and arrows or chopping down trees with axes made from stones. It had never occurred to me that, where there were cavemen, you would have cave women, cave children and cave babies. What would they do all day?

I was certainly wrong about one thing: the hunters all had long spears and could throw them furthest and fastest with special spear-throwers that worked just like those ball-throwers you use when you are throwing a ball for your dog to chase. No one had bows and arrows.

I thought it was time to go home but Neria said:

"There's no hurry. We'll get back at the right time whenever we start. Anyway I want to make you some better clothes: boys clothes that fit you properly."

She said she needed two things: some good, soft animal skins and a lot of thread. The thread looked a bit like very thin string and she said that it was made from nettle-stalks. She had to borrow a sharp knife, which had its blade made from a row of very sharp flakes of stone slotted into a wooden handle, and a needle made from a piece of bone with a hole cut at one end for the thread to go through.

She said we had to go to get the skins from the men who turned new skins, just off a dead animal, into nice soft leather. She warned me it would be very smelly over there because of the way it was done. She was right - as we got near to some men working with skins near a very small pond the smell was awful: like a mix of a dead rabbit that was going rotten and a public toilet that hadn't been cleaned out for months.

"That's the wee pond" said Neria proudly. "All the men and boys stand at the edge and wee into it. Then the skins are soaked in wee until they are soft and it's easy to scrape the hair off."

I asked if they washed the wee off afterwards.

"Yes, but they have to do something else first. When we kill an animal we eat nearly all of it but we don't eat the brains. The men rub the brains into the wee-wet skins and that stops them going rotten and after a few more days you can clean the skins and they are lovely and soft, just right to make you some clothes."

I said "Oh good."

She started measuring me with sticks and drawing a pattern on the skins with a stick that was burnt at one end and worked like a pencil.

By the time we had fed the babies again and had our mid-day meal with everyone else, I said I really wanted to get back home. Neria said she would leave my new clothes with her Mum and finish them when we came back next time. I thought that was a good idea: the smell might have gone by then with any luck.

We were soon back by the hot springs and got clean by swimming, before I got dressed in my own clothes, and we went down the hill to home.

Mum asked "Did you have a nice time and do anything interesting?"

"We had a nice swim" we both said at once.

Things to think about

- What do today's babies eat when they are just starting to eat solid food?
- Is it wrong to eat frogs?
- Do you think we still use wee and brains to make soft leather? Can you find out what we do use?
- If you visited Neria's world would it be scary, exciting, cold, smelly, dangerous, fun?

Chapter 7 Electricity – wild and tamed

As soon as we were back at my home, Neria started asking about "The Electricity Magic" – she really wanted to understand how all the "magic" worked but there weren't many of her questions that I could answer myself. There was one I could try:

She asked "Why isn't there any electricity in my world?".

I told her I thought there was – "Do you remember that storm when we were going to bed?"

"Yes, but that was just a flash and a loud bang. It often happens."

"Well, the flash is electricity jumping from the sky to the ground. It's kind of wild electricity and quite dangerous, lightning killed one of our cows once. The tame electricity we keep in wires is connected to the things we want to work. The electricity is still a bit dangerous if it gets out, so the wires have stuff round them that electricity can't get through and that keeps it in. If you take an electric machine apart the electricity can get out and might hurt you."

Dad suggested we went round the house and found all the different things that used electricity and see what they did. Electric lights you could switch on and off were everywhere but lots of the more complicated machines were in the kitchen. Then there were the things with screens you could watch.

When Neria and I had found more than fifty things you could switch on and off, she asked me to show her how to make electricity (or did you catch wild electricity and tame it like we had animals)?

I knew it had to be made but had no idea how it was done, so we asked Dad.

He told us to come with him when he went to fetch the cows for milking and he would show us some ways of making electricity.

He asked us "What are those things up on the roof of the barn?"

They looked like windows on the sloping roof of the barn. Lots of them, side-by-side, but you couldn't see through them or open them.

I said "I'd forgotten about them, they make electricity when the sun shines on them. I don't know how they do it though."

Dad said he didn't know either. They were clever inventions and didn't need any moving bits to work.

He said "I suppose it's a bit like the leaf of a plant when the sun shines on it. The leaf makes energy that keeps the plant alive but the solar panels make electricity which is just a different sort of energy."

Dad said that the other ways of making electricity had to have moving bits because spinning a magnet around inside a coil of wire was the easiest way of making electricity. When we got home I had to show Neria what magnets were and let her play with them but first Dad pointed out a wind turbine a long way up the valley near where the people from the next-door farm live.

“That makes electricity by turning round magnets quite fast when the wind blows well. It only makes a small amount of electricity – just enough for the one house and only when the wind is blowing.”

Finally he pointed out the line of huge pylons that held up six thick wires going across the valley.

“Where do you think they come from?” I said “Isn't there a big lake at the top of that valley?” and Dad said I was right.

“The lake was made by building a big dam across the valley and there are long pipes that carry the water down to where they make the electricity. The water whooshes out of the pipe like a waterfall and turns huge wheels that turn the magnets. It makes lots and lots of electricity - enough for a small town. That's where the wires go. You can choose when to let the water go down the pipes so you get the electricity just when you want it.”

Neria had been interested in trying to understand what Dad said but she soon realised that it would never work in her world.

“We haven't got wires, we haven't got magnets, we haven't even got metal to make the wires. I think, when I'm grown up, I'll try to find a way of taming wild electricity. But it might be more use to tame some wild animals.”

Things to think about

- Count how many things are electric in your kitchen. What do they all do?
- What electric things are there in your bedroom?
- Is the electricity that works a torch dangerous?
- What are the old-fashioned ways of making electricity - ways we are trying to give-up to stop the world getting too hot?
- Can you explain to Neria how mobile phones work?
- If Neria ever does find out how to tame animals, what sort of animal will probably be the one she and her people tame first?

Chapter 8 Shopping and hunting

We shared my bed again last night but I think Neria's getting a bit less scared about sleeping on her own. Perhaps she'll stay in my room but use her own bed tonight.

As soon was we had eaten breakfast Mum said she was going shopping and that we couldn't come. Because of the pandemic the shops only let one person from each car do the shopping.

Neria asked what shopping was and I said Mum was going out to get something to eat.

Neria replied "You mean she's going hunting? Hunting doesn't work very well if you are on your own. Can't we all go?"

I tried to explain about shopping and how you give the shop money in exchange for what you want. Neria didn't know what money was and said:

"If someone visits us and has got something we want, like salt for preserving fish or red powder for painting with, we take it and give him some of our fur skins."

I said that was a bit like using money but more difficult because you had to find someone who had what you wanted and wanted what you had. With money all you had to find was someone who had what you wanted. Then they could use your money to buy what they wanted from someone else. I showed her some coins and she thought they were very pretty. She said if she had some she would make them into a necklace not swap them for salt.

So I gave her ten one-centime coins to keep.

Mum said that, as we couldn't go with her, we could walk along the farm lane and meet her when she was coming back.

Neria saw Mum leaving in the car. "What's that? Is it a sort of animal you've tamed? Or does electricity make it go?"

So now I needed to explain how cars work. It's not easy when the person you are teaching doesn't even understand what wheels are. I took her to see our little tractor where it is easier to see its insides than with a car. Dad even started it and let me drive it across the field. Neria was most impressed.

Once the tractor was back in its barn, Neria and I set off along the farm lane to the road Mum would come along on her way back from the shops. Neria spotted a dead rabbit that had been killed by a car but not squashed flat. She seemed really pleased: "Now I can make a nice meal for you all".

Mum didn't seem really pleased about Neria's rabbit but she let her bring it home in the car. Neria asked if she could cook it in the garden "I don't know how to use all the electric things in your kitchen." Mum thought a barbecue would be much better than an indoor meal, so Neria started work and wanted me to help.

Neria issued the instructions "I'll get the fire going. Have you got a cooking pot? When you've got it, you can skin and gut the rabbit while I find some vegetables."

I didn't think this was a very good idea: I'd never skinned and gutted anything and I wasn't sure I wanted to. So I said "I know where all the best vegetables grow: you do the rabbit and I'll find the vegetables." First I got her a really big iron pot which we use for barbecue meals. She was most impressed.

"It's really strong, I'm sure it won't break like our clay ones keep doing."

It didn't take long to get the vegetables: I just went to Mum's kitchen garden and dug up some potatoes and carrots and picked some beans. Neria was amazed at how quick I had been and had never seen potatoes before. Our beans and carrots were much bigger and juicer than the wild ones she ate at home.

She had got on well with skinning the rabbit. She had borrowed one of Mum's sharp knives ("much sharper than my flint ones") and cut slits in the skin without cutting right through to the rabbit's insides. Then she sort of peeled the skin off like a Mum taking a Baby-Grow off a baby, just leaving it with booties, mittens and a bonnet. When it was undressed, the rabbit still had fur socks on its feet and fur all over its head. My Granny used to say "Skin a rabbit" when she was getting you ready for a bath. Now I know why.

Then Neria cut into the rabbit's tummy and took out all the slimy, smelly bits but she sorted out the liver and heart and kidneys and put them in the cooking pot with all the meaty bits of the rabbit.

I washed my vegetables and cut them up before putting them in with the rabbit. When the water had been added, I asked if we should put in some salt.

She explained "Salt's much too valuable to use in a stew. It's just for making fish and meat last right through the winter without going rotten."

Then she suggested "Why don't you get some of those wild garlic leaves from your little wood? They'll make it taste nice."

We soon had the fire going well, thanks to my magic matches, and about an hour and a half later the meal was ready. We used plates and knives and forks – I had already taught Neria how we used them. Mum and Dad ate lots and I think they were telling the truth when they said the rabbit stew was really good. They asked what we had made for pudding.

Neria said "There's loads of blackberries on those bramble bushes. We always eat them as we pick them, it's easier like that."

After our meal we could escape to go up the hill to check the sheep and have a swim. Well that's what we told Mum and Dad but I think we might fit in another trip to Neria's home.

I hope so anyway.

Things to think about

- Would Édouard use the same money as us?
- How would you explain how a car works to Neria?
- Have you ever eaten a wild animal?
- If Neria takes the ten pretty coins home with her what will her parents and friends think they are?
- Why hadn't Neria ever seen potatoes before?`

Chapter 9 Becoming a Goat

As we were climbing up the hill Neria explained that she wanted to spend a few days with her tribe. The days were getting a lot shorter and it was time for a big party and special ceremonies to make sure the gods would send plenty of food for winter.

I said that sounded like fun and I didn't mind staying because I knew I'd get back home at the same time that it was now. So we made our way through the cave and into Neria's world for my third visit.

Of course it was just the same time as when we had left Neria's world and the bits of leather she had been making into a set of clothes for me were still there and still just as smelly as they had been when we left.

Neria said it was really important to have some nice clothes for the party and she could get rid of the smell when the clothes were made.

It took her most of the day to make my clothes, with some help from her Mum, and then she washed them without actually getting them soaking wet and dried them near the fire with the smoke blowing all over them. They smelt quite nice afterwards.

While she had been making my clothes I had gone exploring. There was a little group of men sitting around a pile of stones. One man sorted through the stones very carefully and chose just one, then he hit it with another stone and a big piece chipped off leaving a fairly sharp edge on one side and a thicker bit you could hold on the other. He told me it was a scraper that he needed to scrape the fat and bits of meat off the animal skins before they were soaked in the wee pond.

When my new clothes were made Neria wanted me to try them. First she gave me a pair of fur pants and a fur vest - she hadn't made those herself, they were spare ones her Mum had. She said "it's getting cold at this time of year - you need some beaver fur underneath your clothes. Beaver fur is really the best for keeping warm."

The leather clothes went on top beautifully and were really comfortable.

Neria said "Now all they need is painting with your animal god".

I'd noticed that most people had pictures of animals on their shirts and wondered how it was done.

Neria asked "What animal is your special god?" and I said I didn't know.

She replied "You can share mine."

Her animal was a wild goat that we call a bouquetin in French. She lit a stick in the fire and got it burning at one end. Then she blew out the flames but left it glowing red while she drew the goat on my shirt. The drawing wasn't the soot from the stick, the glowing stick burnt the skin a bit so the picture of the goat should last for ever.

When it was done. Neria said "Now the goat god will look after both of us."

It was getting near to meal time and I asked Neria what we would have this evening.

She said "It's the children's turn to hunt again but it's not frogs this time. It's grasshoppers – I ought to have been helping to catch them instead of making your clothes."

There were absolutely thousands of grasshoppers jumping and chirping in the long grass around Neria's home but I had never thought you could eat them. The other children had a competition to see who could catch the most: every child had a little leather bag to collect them in and then held the top shut to stop them jumping out. Cooking them was easy: the grown-ups heated really big flat stones in the fire and then slid them out to the edge of the fire. The children each poured their grasshoppers on the hot stones and they crackled and popped until they were cooked. Eating them wasn't so easy: you had to break them in half and peel off their shells. Inside the meat was nicely cooked and tasted really good – a bit like the shrimps we had cooked at the sea-side when I was little.

When it was bedtime Neria and I tucked ourselves up together under the skin blankets near the fire, like we had last time. This time I tried hard to understand the story that one of the men told. I must have learned a bit more of Neria's language because I could understand what he was saying. This is the story he told:

In the beginning the Gods lived in the heavens with the stars. The Sun God and Moon God carried their torches as they searched amongst the stars for something interesting to do.

Eventually they got bored and thought "there must be something more exciting than stars" and decided to take a look at the Earth.

"That'll be a waste of time" said the Moon "it's dark and flat and dead and horrid."

The Sun said it was worth a try and both decided to leave their huge torches circling in the sky near Earth so they could see where they were going. When the Sun God's torch was shining it was really bright daytime. Night-time was when you had the Moon God's torch or, sometimes, just the stars.

The Earth was flat, so the two gods made it more interesting by making high mountains and deep valleys.

Then they said "It still doesn't do anything" and thought some more.

What they thought was "Rain". They made it rain for days on end, really hard. The rain filled the valleys and hollows and made rivers and lakes. On the tops of the mountains the rain was snow instead of rain.

"We need some things that move about and do things, to make it really interesting" said the gods.

So they made lots of animals: fish in the rivers, frogs in the ponds and lots of furry animals and birds all over the place. And the first thing the animals all said to the gods was:

"We are hungry, please give us something to eat" so the gods covered the land with grass and moss and trees and

lots of other plants and most of the animals had plants to eat and were content. Some of them decided they did not like their plants and ate other animals instead and the Gods were not very pleased with them. They didn't destroy them though, they just left them alone to see what would happen and whether the animals would get it all sorted out for themselves.

Sometimes, just for fun, a god would go to live inside an animal to see what it was like and to make the animal learn to do new things.

Gods cannot have children themselves and when they saw all the animals breeding and taking over the Earth they decided they wanted children too. Gods are spirits so the only way they could make a new god was to put part of their spirit into an animal and let it live there, learning about the Earth, until the animal itself died. Then the spirit could join its relations in the spirit world of the gods.

The gods wanted a really good animal to raise their spirit children so they made a new kind, a clever one that could make tools and clothes and talk easily to each other and eat lots of different things. And as a present the gods gave them fire.

And from that time to this the gods have mostly kept themselves hidden from the people. But they are there and the people have slowly learned more about them. And the people know that they are the children of the gods and one day will become god spirits themselves. Meanwhile, everyone must respect and worship their ancestors who are already gods in the spirit world.

It was a great story but I thought it was a fairy tale to tell at bedtime. I asked Neria if it were true.

"Of course it is, sometimes we can talk to the spirits of our ancestors and the animals and if we make the gods happy they make sure the animals don't all migrate away from us when we need them for food. That story told me how the world started and where people came from and what will happen when I die. It's a really important story."

Before she went to sleep, Neria said "I'll show you tomorrow how we talk to the spirits of the animals - you'll enjoy it."

It sounds like tomorrow might be interesting.

"Good night, Neria."

Things to think about

- Why is beaver fur the best for keeping you warm in winter?
- Édouard watched a man make a scraper out of stone. What other useful tools might Neria's people make that way?
- If a story helps you think about important things, does it matter if it's exactly true or not?
- Would you like to taste a grasshopper?

Chapter 10 A Painted Party

Next morning Neria said the party to see the animal spirits would happen this afternoon and she wanted to show me how to paint the animal spirits first. She got two little leather bags with dry powdered earth - one red, one black and she led me to a small cave not far from the big cave where we slept.

"Even children like me can practise painting here - it's not like the secret cave where the real spirit paintings are."

The first paintings we saw were some hands.

She said "These are really easy to do, I'll show you."

She sucked some of the red powder into her mouth, pressed one of her hands on the wall of the cave and blew all the red powder on to the back of her hand. When she took her hand away, there was a picture of her hand, the same colour as the wall of the cave but outlined by all the red powder on the wall near the hand. There were lots of hand-prints just like it, all over the walls.

She said "You have a try" so I sucked some black powder into my mouth and made a black hand print beside her red one.

She said "Doing animals is much more difficult but it doesn't matter if you just practise here. We are still in the light and the rain blows in, so all the paintings we children do disappear quite quickly. Not like the secret ones we'll see this afternoon - I think they'll last for ever.

We decided she should try to draw a goat because we each had the sign of the Goat God on our jerkins. Neria didn't blow the paint on this time but mixed the powder with some fat and spread it on with her fingers. She's a really good goat artist..

It was still morning when we had finished the painting. The midday meal was going to be a special one, before the cave-party, and lots of the grown-ups were getting it ready. We just sat near the fire and watched, or sometimes we just looked at each other and smiled. I'd had an itchy head all day and kept on scratching until Neria said:

"You've got lice, well so have I – everybody has them. Sit still and I'll de-louse you." She sat behind me and I could feel her fingers combing through my hair. It was a nice feeling and I just went into a dream until, every so often, she'd say "got one".

Then it was my turn to search her hair but not before she had shown me how to pop a louse between your thumb and finger nails. I didn't catch as many as she had but she seemed to enjoy being searched just like I had. I suddenly remembered seeing a television programme about baboons in Africa and they spent a long time searching each other's fur and obviously enjoying it. Well now I know what it's like to be a baboon.

The meal was later than usual but worth waiting for. We started with boiled eggs - two each. They weren't as big as hen's eggs and Neria said the were from the nests of a sort of grouse that goes white in winter. She must mean ptarmigan, we've still got a few that live in the mountains near my home but they are ever so rare.

Then there was a deer (a red deer not a reindeer) that had a pole stuck right through it and the deer had been moved round on its pole as it cooked, so it was well cooked right through. There weren't any cooked vegetables just a salad of dandelion leaves, but we finished off with blackberries. We didn't have to pick our own, this time someone had picked a whole basketful and roasted them at the edge of the fire so they were all hot and juicy.

Then it was time for the secret cave. Most of the grown-ups made burning torches like Neria had used on my first visit to her world. Some had drums or little flutes made of hollow bones. It wasn't the cave where we lived that we were going to but one high up on the side of the valley. It took us half-an-hour to get to the entrance and then another half hour stooping and crawling along a tunnel until we got to a big cavern and the torches were fixed on the walls. Then we could see an amazing sight.

All around the cavern walls and ceiling were paintings of animals and lots of them looked almost alive. They looked even more alive as the party got going: people were drumming and making strange tunes with their bone flutes. Some were dancing. The torches flickered and the flickering and shadows made the paintings come alive and start moving. The old man who had told the story about the Sun and Moon Gods started talking to the animals and asking them not to go away during the winter.

"Although we must eat some of you we know your spirits will join the gods and your children will live happy lives. It is the will of the gods that we share the world and each live our own lives."

The music and the dancing had left people tired but happy. They hugged each other and kissed. And then it was time to go back to the real world outside.

Neria told me "We won't go back to the cave until Spring when we say thank you to the gods for making the plants start growing again and the animals to start breeding."

I said "Shall we go back to my house? It's warmer there and we can each have a shampoo to get rid of the rest of our lice."

"What's a shampoo, Édouard?"

Things to think about

- Have you ever had lice? How did your parents get rid of them?
- Why do you think Neria's tribe kept the cave with the paintings a secret?
- Do you think most wild animals wish there weren't any people or wolves or lions or bears?

Chapter 11 A Bath and a Book and a Dog

When we got back to the cave we both changed out of our leather clothes and put on the jeans and tee-shirts we wore in my world. I'd left my old leather clothes with Neria's Mum so it was my new clothes with the goat picture that I left hidden in the cave along with Neria's clothes with the same goat picture. It made me feel as though I was really part of her family clan too.

Back home I asked Mum if we could have a bath. She looked at us and seemed a bit surprised at my request but then she looked at us again and said:

"I think that's a very good idea, there's plenty of hot water so you can have a bath each, without waiting for the water to warm-up again."

I showed Neria how to turn the bath taps and the shower on and off and found the old bottle of louse shampoo that Mum had used on me.

Then I went to my bedroom (well I suppose it's our bedroom now) and found a book to read while Neria tried to drown her lice.

Neria re-appeared, wrapped-up in a big towel and I told her to sit on her bed while her hair got try and while I had my bath.

"Read one of my books while you get dry if you like."

"What's reading?"

When I came back, wrapped in my towel, Neria was looking through a book. She was turning the pages and looking at the pictures. It was a book about dogs.

"Did you make these paintings Édouard? Like I did the goat in the cave?"

I told her that I couldn't draw that well and anyway these were photos - like the one she had taken of me with my magic phone .

"I didn't know you had tame wolves in this world. Have you got one? Can I play with it?"

I explained that we had a special word for tame wolves: we called them dogs.

"Yes, we've got one. She's called Moonlight and she's our sheep-dog so she doesn't live in the house like most dogs do. She sleeps in our barn - the one that's got all those electricity panels on its roof."

After breakfast Neria said simply "Where's your wolf?" So I took her out to the barn and let Moonlight out.

She bounced around, tail-wagging, and tried to lick each of us. Neria was entranced, she had never met an animal that actually liked people before. Moonlight didn't even mind when Neria put her hand in the dog's mouth so she could see and feel its teeth.

"They are just like a wolf's teeth - she ought to be a really fierce animal. Why isn't she?"

"It's like the cows. Dogs have lived with humans for hundreds of years. They probably think they are humans or that we are the boss dogs in their pack."

It was time to check the sheep and we decided Moonlight could come with us. I don't usually take her because you don't need a sheepdog when all the sheep are safely in their own field. Also she is a nuisance when you wanted a swim.

Of course the sheep were still safely in their field but we went through the gate so I could show Neria how my tame wolf hunted sheep. I whistled the same way Dad does and Moonlight ran to round-up the sheep and got them all together in one corner of the field and then she lay down looking at them. If one tried to wander off, she got up and chased it back to the flock.

Neria said "I want a tame wolf - think how easy it would be to hunt deer if you had a wolf to round them up like that. Let's go to my home and try to tame a wolf."

I wasn't sure this would work but Neria wouldn't change her mind, so we changed into our leather goat clothes and went through the cave.

Neria's Dad was carving a piece of bone into a really good model of a deer. He said he was fit it to his spear-thrower to bring him luck when next he went hunting. Spears get broken quite often but spear-throwers last a long time so it's worth making a really nice carving to go on them.

Neria interrupted her Dad: "Come on, you can finish the carving tomorrow I want you to catch me a wolf-cub."

Her Dad explained that they only hunted wolves in the winter when their fur was really thick and made warm clothes.

Neria interrupted to say "I don't want a dead wolf to make some new knickers, I want a live baby one I can tame and teach to hunt for us."

Her Dad said "Well it's the right time of year for wolf cubs but they stay in their dens so I don't know how we could catch one. Why don't you come hunting with us after our meal and we'll see if we can spot any wolves. You'll need to be careful and let me and the other men go in front – you haven't got spears and we might need them."

So after lunch Neria's Dad and five other men set off for a hunt with me and Neria following along well behind them.

The gods must have been on our side that day. We found a herd of bison most of which ran away before we got close but one must have been hurt and was limping and couldn't run fast. The men crept up and soon had it speared. When it was dead the men joked with us: "Why don't you carry it home for us?" Of course we couldn't move it an inch let alone pick it up, so four of the men fixed it on a pole and set off to take it home.

Neria's Dad said "Come on, two men aren't enough for hunting but let's see if we can find a wolf cub."

We followed the bison tracks up the hill until we got to where the snow started. There were the bison that had run away from the hunters and a pack of wolves were closing in on them. Neria's Dad said "We don't want wolves killing all our bison, let's chase them away."

So we did but we also chased away the bison by mistake.

Neria's Dad said "Come on kids, it's time to go home and get that bison skinned."

We were just setting off when Neria spotted a little animal outside its burrow. It was a wolf cub.

We grabbed it and took it home with us.

"It can eat some bison meat" said Neria but she was wrong. It was too small and needed its mother's milk. Neria was afraid it would die but eventually she persuaded her big sister, who had a baby of her own, to let the wolf-cub share some of her milk.

A week later the puppy started eating the chewed-up meat we gave the bigger babies. Neria called her Kumia and she was soon friends with everyone and ate the meat people threw to her while they were eating their own meal.

We had been in Neria's world for well over a week and I wanted to go home. Neria knew we'd be back with her wolf cub in no time at all, so she didn't mind coming with me.

When we got out of the cave in our normal clothes Moonlight was still guarding the sheep and hadn't noticed we had been away. We went straight home but we should have had a swim first. As soon as Mum saw us she said:

"How did you get this dirty, it was only yesterday you both had a bath."

We said we'd been playing with a puppy. I suppose spending over a week in Neria's world does leave you a bit dirty. We both had another bath that night.

Things to think about

- Do dogs in our world think they are still wolves? or humans? or just dogs?
- There are hundreds of different sorts of dog, big, small, fluffy or smooth, long pointed muzzles or short faces. As soon as a baby is starting to talk it says “dog” whatever sort of dog it sees. How does the baby know that they are all dogs and not cats?
- Would you like to go hunting bison? Or is it cruel? What could Neria’s people eat if they didn’t hunt animals?
- Do you eat animals? Who kills them?

Chapter 12 Reading a story

When we woke up it was pouring with rain and when we had eaten our breakfast it was still pouring with rain, only harder. Dad said the rain would last all day and we needn't go and check the sheep – he'd do it, because he needed to go and check the heifers himself.

"Why don't you have a quiet day in your room and read some stories?"

So we went back up to our room. Neria chose a book with a picture of some dogs on the cover. She looked inside and was obviously disappointed.

"Where are the pictures of more dogs? It's all just little black squiggles that don't mean anything."

I told her they were words.

"Rubbish" she replied "words are sounds that you say not squiggles you see in a book."

So I had to try and explain reading and writing and it's not easy.

I pointed out the letters and explained that each one meant a sound that made part of a word. Like D O G making "dog". I also said that learning to read and write is hard work – you need a teacher and lots of practise.

"When a baby learns to walk it also starts to learn to talk. You don't have to teach a baby to walk and talk, it just does it and you can't stop it even if you wanted to. It only learns to read when it's older and someone teaches it. I could teach you if you want."

She soon realised that would be a waste of time.

"In my world no one can read or write so I wouldn't have anything to read and if I wrote something no one would be able to read it. Reading's a silly idea I think."

I didn't agree:

"Reading is great, you can have whatever story you want, whenever you want it, even if you are on your own. And you can have stories from thousands of years ago or far distant lands."

I picked a book off my shelf and said "I think you'll like this story. It was written more than two thousand years ago in a language called Latin and now it's been turned into French so I can read it."

I started to read her the tale of Romulus and Remus:

Rhea Silvia was the daughter of King Numitor but his nasty brother Amulius chased him out of the country and took over as King.

When Rhea Silvia had twin boys, and some people said their father was the God Mars, Amulius was afraid that the boys would grow up and take back their grandfather Numitor's place as king. So Amulius stole the twins and left them out one cold night on the banks of the river Tiber where they would freeze and die.

The baby twins were found by a mother wolf and she picked up the twins and took them back to her den to feed them to her cubs. But she didn't, the twins and the cubs cuddled up together and kept each other warm and the mother wolf let the twins, as well as her own cubs, drink her milk and share their food until they were big and strong.

As young men, Romulus and Remus found their grandfather Numitor and helped him defeat Amulius and become king again.

Then Romulus and Remus, now young princes, wanted to build a new city but they disagreed about the best place to build it, they had a fight and Remus was killed. So Romulus could choose where the city would be built and it was named after him – Rome, the city of Romulus.

Neria's first question was "What's a city?" and I had some more explaining to do.

Then she said "One bit of your story is like my story but the other way round. I found a wolf cub and my sister let it drink her milk until it was old enough to eat. In your story it's two boys who get found by a she-wolf and drink her milk."

Then she went on "You don't need books to have stories from long, long ago. My Grandma and Grandad told me stories they had been told by their grandparents. I'll tell them to my children and grandchildren one day. You don't need to be able to read, just able to remember and everyone can do that."

She was right of course and I was quite glad. I'd learnt Neria's language but I would need to learn how to write it down if she could read. I'll learn her stories and how to do all the things that she can do by just listening and watching and talking.

It was lunch time – cheese sandwiches, apples and a drink of water. It was still raining but Neria suggested we go out to the stone barn where Mum and Dad make the cheese and keep the balls of cheese on racks until they are ready to eat. She really wants to learn how to make cheese, she thinks it will be much more useful than writing.

Neria said "I bet it's not raining in my world, let's go and see if I'm right."

So we told Mum we wanted a walk in the rain and she said:

"OK but don't be too long and you'll need a nice warm bath when you get back."

So we set off up the hill to change clothes in the cave and see what would happen next in Neria's world.

We left Moonlight guarding the sheep. I didn't need to guess what we would find when we walked out of the cave and into Neria's world. It was exactly the same time as when we had left and Neria's wolf-cub Kumia was playing with the other children and hadn't even noticed we had gone. The adults didn't notice us slinking off and then reappearing either – they probably just thought we had gone for a wee.

Things to think about

- Why is reading and writing so important to us but not important at all in Neria's world?
- What book have you read that was written more than 1000 years ago?
- Could you explain to Neria how to make cheese?
- When you read a story, how do you decide whether it is true or just a made-up story?

Chapter 13 The Salt Man and his Wolves

On my last visit to Neria's world I had spent more than a week living with her clan of friends and relations. Mostly they were relations – loads of different relations, cousins, aunts, uncles, grandparents as well as Neria's brother and sister and her Mum and Dad. Anyway, I knew them all now and was friendly with almost everyone. It was only the old man who liked telling stories about the gods and the beginning of the world who seemed to expect children always to be very polite and not noisy. None of us kids liked him much.

This time it wasn't just Neria's big family that welcomed us, Kumia, Neria's wolf cub, was still there – she hadn't noticed we'd been away any more than the humans had.

That afternoon something most unusual happened: a visitor arrived. It was quite rare for a visitor to come from just the next cave clan a few miles away. This visitor had come from the seaside a hundred miles away and he had two tame wolves with him. Neria was a bit disappointed: she had thought she was the first person in her world to think of taming a wolf. She told me Argider came every year at this time to swap bags of salt for our best beaver skins.

"He didn't have tame wolves when he came last time though."

Having a visitor was really important for everyone: the salt was needed for the autumn so that fish and meat could be preserved for winter but just as important, it was an excuse for a party. We made a really good meal (reindeer, Argider said they were rare where he came from) and afterwards we listened to all his stories.

Apart from me, no one except Argider had seen the sea and they all found it difficult to believe what he told them about a huge lake that was so big you couldn't see the other side and where the water was all salty. He made the salt by drying seawater with fires or in the sun. Neria thought it was all a fairy story until I told her it was true and that we might be able to go to the seaside in my world when Mum and Dad were allowed to drive long distances in their car again.

Neria asked where Argider had got his tame wolves.

"I swapped them for some salt - one of the tribes three day's march away from here reared a pair of cubs like you did and when the cubs were old enough they started breeding. So they had these two really friendly cubs spare and gave them to me."

Neria wanted to breed more tame wolves and said "I need a male cub too." and Argider said:

"When I come back next year will be soon enough for Kumia to start breeding and I will have a male wolf with me."

Neria was already dreaming of having a whole pack of tame wolves and encouraged Argider to tell more stories about his two wolves.

Argider said they were really helpful with hunting. When it was just him and his two wolves he would hide as close as he could get to the animal he wanted to kill, then the wolves would creep up on the animal and, quite often, it would run away from the wolves and get close enough to him for him to spear it.

Then he told story about when he hunted with some friends from the clan that had given him his own wolves. Five men and six wolves had managed to chase some bison and scared them so much that the fell off the top of a cliff and were all killed. It took ages to carry them home and invite enough people from all around to the party where all the bison were cooked and eaten.

But his best wolf story was about how they had saved him from being eaten. He said that far, far away were people who thought the gods permitted people to eat other people. They didn't eat their friends, just enemies from other tribes that they captured or killed in battle.

Argider was captured by a band of six cannibals and was being marched off towards the cannibals' cave. The wolves slunk along some way behind Argider and at the right moment he whistled for them to come and then screamed and pointed at the rapidly approaching wolves. The cannibals ran off as fast as they could and Argider escaped the other way, back to where his own clan lived.

Argider's stories seemed to get less believable as the evening went on but everyone was enjoying them and seemed pleased that he was willing to stay for a few more days.

Neria told me it was the time of year when the salmon came –that was why everyone was so pleased that Argider had brought all that salt. Usually there are quite small numbers of fairly small fish in the river. You can catch them in the basketwork fish traps or stand, dead-still, at the edge of the river, like a heron, and stab the fish with your fishing spear.

When the salmon come, there are hundreds of huge fish swimming up the river and jumping to climb the waterfalls. They are really easy to catch, children can do it with their hands sometimes. The only problem is all the bears that come fishing too: you need to find somewhere where the bears aren't too close.

It was impossible to eat the salmon as fast as we could catch them, so everyone had to take turns cutting the salmon open, cleaning out their guts and then rubbing salt into their flesh so they will last all winter without going rotten.

When we ran out of salt we started smoking the fish over the fire instead.

When the salmon-run was over, Argider wanted to go home and Neria's cousin Urraca decided to go with him.

Neria told me "She's three years older than me, I expect she'll have a baby if she comes back with Argider next year."

I had noticed that some of the girls with babies were very young compared to my world.

I was getting quite used to being one of Neria's clan – I'd been there for almost three weeks and now I wanted to go home again. Neria said she'd come too :

"No one will notice I've gone away will they?"

It was still raining when we had changed our clothes and come out of the cave. Moonlight bounded over to great us. We were soaking wet when we got home and that was how Mum had expected us to be. She sent us off for a bath to warm up – she didn't seem to notice how dirty we were after three weeks in Neria's world.

Things to think about

- If you lived in Neria's world would you be afraid of strangers or really pleased to see them?
- Apart from using salt, how else might people have kept food from going rotten?
- Could all Argider's stories be true?
- How old do girls have to be before they can have babies?

Chapter 14 Counting to a million

Another wet day. Even when I wasn't at school Mum and Dad liked me to do some calculations now and again and I quite enjoyed doing them but not quite as much as reading stories to Neria. Even though Neria couldn't write down numbers she could work things out in her head just as easily as I could. Quite often she could beat me to the answer.

By now we both knew that Neria's world was just my world a long time before now. How long? It didn't take long to find the answer on the internet. The people who hunted bison and mammoths and painted animals on cave walls lived about 10,000 or 12,000 thousand years ago, near the end of the Ice Age, when things were getting warmer again but Neria's world was still colder than mine: I already knew that without looking it up on the internet.

We thought about all the people who had lived between Neria's time and now. How many had there been? We decided to try and work it out.

I asked Neria how much older a mother usually was than her baby.

"Well girls usually have their first baby when they are about 15 and don't usually have any more after they are 35 – they are usually grannies by then, so I suppose 25 years older is about average."

I said that people now usually had babies when they were between 20 and 40 so the average was about 30 years in my world.

We wanted to know these details because we imagined a long line of people, each the child of the one behind it in the line, stretching from Neria's time to mine.

If there were 10,000 years between our times and each gap between parent and child was 25 years the line would have 400 people in it. Four hundred generations.

Or maybe Neria's time was 12,000 years ago and the parent child gap was 30 years like it is now. 12,000 divided by 30 also gives 400 generations.

Maybe Neria's sister was my great, great 400-times great grandma. It didn't seem very likely though – or at least it didn't until I talked to Dad about it.

"Dad, how many great grandparents did I have?"

"You should be able to work that out for yourself. There's one of you, you have two parents and four grandparents."

"So it doubles each generation. I must have had eight great grandparents."

"Well done, why do you want to know?"

"Because I want to know how many 400-times great grandparents I had."

"That'll take a bit of counting. Can you count to a million?"

"That would take ages."

"Not if you do it by doubling – I'll show you."

He spread out the fingers of each hand and said "We'll start with one of you."

Then raising his first two fingers "Double it for parents and double it again for grandparents"

He then raised his third finger and got to 8, then he went on doubling and raising fingers: 16, 32, 64, 128, 256, 512, 1024. So in ten steps we had gone from my generation to over 1000 grandparents ten generations ago.

He then asked what would happen in another ten generations starting at 1000 (to keep the counting easy): 2,000, 4,000, 8,000, 16,000, 32,000, 64,000, 128,000, 256,000, 512,000, 1,024,000.

So just using 20 fingers we had counted from one to one million. Another ten generations would take us to one billion grandparents. And we would still have another ten generations to go before we got to Neria's time.

So, once Dad had explained it like this, it was obvious that Neria's sister would have almost certainly have been one of my 400-times great grandparents and so would everyone else in Europe, and maybe elsewhere in the world, (except for people who had never had any children of course).

What if Neria goes back to live in her world and has children when she is old enough? Will I have to call her "Granny 400"?

Neria wanted to get back home for another visit. "You'll feel at home too, now that you know we are all your relations. I suppose it does mean that I can never have a baby with you or you would be your own 400-times great grandfather!" I

I'd never thought about things like that – feeding babies was fun but I didn't fancy being a Dad anytime soon.

Things to think about

- How many of your four grand-parents and eight great grand-parents have you actually met? What do you know about their work and lives?
- If you went back five million years what would your ancestors look like? And if you went back 70 million years (to when there were dinosaurs)?
- Does Édouard think Neria is just his friend, or is like a sister, or is his ancestor?

Chapter 15 A trip to the seaside

Neria was happy to be back with all her relations (and mine too I suppose) and even happier to have Kumia to play with and take for walks hunting, but not quite catching, rabbits.

Neria's Dad decided he wanted to go and see the sea which Argider, the salt man, had told us about. He wanted to bring back some more salt but mainly he wanted an adventure - like Neria, he had never seen the sea. He said Neria could come but not Kumia.

Neria complained "Why not? She might save us from cannibals like Argider's wolves."

Her Dad pointed out that one wolf cub would not scare many cannibals and that she wouldn't be able to walk all the way to the sea.

Argider had told us that the way to get to the sea was simply to follow a river downstream. The river would get wider and wider until it got to the sea. I knew this was true - the little rivers near my home joined the Garonne and then got to the sea at the eastern end of the mountains. Neria's Dad thought it would be better to follow a different river, one that went south to warmer lands and a warmer sea: that is what Argider had told him to do.

So we started by climbing up the mountains and down on what was the Spanish side in my world. From there it took us more than a week of walking everyday before we got to the sea.

We didn't have to carry much with us, no skins and poles to make shelters but just a few extra layers of clothes and some dried meat. Argider had told us that we would meet other clans of people spread out half a day's march or so from each other and that they would be friendly. He was right: we were always welcomed, given plenty of food and had story telling sessions where we described where we had been and they told us all their news.

We played with their children. Playing with Neria's friends I had already noticed that most of the games were just the same as the ones we played in my world: hide-and-seek, tag and skimming stones for example. Here, even though we were in Spain, the games were the same and so was the language with just a slightly different accent. Everyone could understand each other easily.

But there was one game that was new: cannibals. Most of the children hid and tried to avoid being caught by the two or three "cannibals". If they were caught, everyone would pretend to cook and eat them.

This wasn't just a children's game, the adults told us that sometimes a cannibal tribe from the other side of the river came across to hunt people and not just wild animals. We hadn't really believed Argider's story about being rescued from cannibals by his tame wolves but now we did so we were careful to keep a good look-out for dangerous looking hunters. Even if we had brought Kumia, we only had one tame wolf and she was quite small, so she would be no good at scaring off cannibals.

We didn't meet any cannibals and each day we were welcomed by friendly groups of people who lived on our side of the river. As the river got bigger the people's lives got more linked in with the river. They made little boats which were really big woven baskets made with willow twigs just like an ordinary basket but with animal skins stretched over the outside of the basket and greased with fat to make them waterproof.

The little boats enabled people to catch fish on both sides of the river, put their fish-traps in the best places and hunt otters and beavers for their beautiful warm furs.

At last we got to the sea and met up with Argider and his clan of salt-makers and fishermen. Neria's cousin Urraca was part of his clan now and told us, proudly, that she would have his baby in about five or six months time.

We stayed with Argider for about a month learning how to make salt and to use the boats made from big, hollowed out tree-trunks that were used in shallow waters to hunt for fish. When we decided to set off for home, Argider gave us as much salt as we could carry in return for all the work we had helped him with.

The homeward journey was easy for the first few days, we knew the way and stayed with the same friendly clans who had been kind to us on our way to the seaside.

On the fifth day of our journey, when we were still a long way from the next friendly clan, a group of six very strange looking hunters stepped out from behind some bushes. They all had spears but the really odd thing about them was their clothes and the fact that one of them was wearing a pair of deer antlers on his head. All six of them had the same picture on their jerkins: part man, part animal with antlers on its head and a tail like a horse. We assumed that it was a god or magician that protected them, like Neria's goat drawing protected us. But our goats didn't seem to be protecting us too well: the men grabbed me and Neria, tied us up with strips of leather and made us sit beside another girl who they had already tied up. Neria's Dad tried his best to rescue us but it was six against one and he was soon caught and tied up too. Then they made us walk in front, still tied on long leads like a dog, while they drove us forward towards what we supposed would be their home cave.

The other girl was crying and told us that we would all be cooked and eaten at the feast these cannibals had every autumn.

"They make themselves look like the evil god they worship" she told us.

I noticed she had a goat drawing on her tunic just like me and Neria - so we should all be protected by him and I just hoped he was a more powerful god than theirs but I was afraid he wasn't - not when it was one adult and three kids against six big cannibals.

I was pleased to see that Neria was not crying and obviously wanted to discuss possible escape plans with me but didn't because the cannibals would hear our plans.

We both stared in all directions trying to find a way to escape when, suddenly, I knew exactly what we had to do. I looked at Neria and signalled her to be quiet, I hope she realised that what I was going to do was an escape plan and that she must let me try to make it work.

I started speaking, as loudly and slowly as I could, so I would seem more important than just a boy.

"We are all guarded by the Goat God and I have summoned him to destroy you. Look up at the sun and you will see that he has already eaten part of it. Goats can eat anything. Watch a little longer and you will see he has eaten some more. When he has eaten all the sun it will be dark forever and you will all die of cold. There is just one thing you can do to survive: let us go and go quickly to your cave and build a fire in honour of the Goat God. You must burn all your antlers and shirts with the antlered devil pictures and make new shirts with images of the Goat God. Do this fast enough and the Goat God will stop eating the sun and let it regrow to full size again."

They watched for another minute and saw the bite out of the sun get bigger as the invisible Goat God munched away. They soon decided to do what I had instructed, they let us go and disappeared over the horizon.

It was about half an hour before the Goat God stopped eating the sun and it started to return to its usual round shape.

The crying girl had stopped crying and was looking at me in awe and almost worship, as though I were a god myself.

Neria said simply "How did you do that? I didn't think you really believed in our gods."

I explained "It doesn't matter what I believe, what mattered is that they believed me. I saw the little nibble out of the circle of the sun and I knew that it was the start of an eclipse, when part of the moon goes in front of part of the sun and hides it. I knew the bit of the sun that was hidden would get bigger and then get smaller again whatever the cannibals did. So I had to get them to believe me quickly and I was lucky."

Neria didn't really believe me: the sun and the moon were both gods and lived in the sky the same distance away. One wasn't going to go in front of the other. It wasn't the time for a science lesson, we needed to comfort the girl who had been crying so recently. She told us her name was Ilara and that her Dad had been killed by the cannibals when they had captured her. Her home was with the clan that we were planning to spend the night with and so we set off to get her home as quickly as possible.

Her Mum was horrified that her man had been killed but so relieved that we had rescued her daughter that she didn't know what to do or say. Everyone treated us as heros for rescuing Ilara and when Neria told her version of the story they all assumed I must be a most powerful magician. I felt a bit guilty about tricking them but really pleased with myself for making the trick work on the cannibals.

When we were safely back at Neria's home the story got told again, in an improved version, by Neria and her Dad so that too many people began to think I must be a real magician or sorcerer. It was getting embarrassing and I wanted to see my parents again (I'd been away for over a month). I asked Neria to come with me:

"I'll tell you the real way I did the trick with the sun when we are in my world."

So we went back though the cave and had a very good swim, to wash off most of the dirt, before going down the hill to home.

Mum met us and asked if we'd had a good day:

"You look cleaner than usual, what have you been up to?"

"We got caught by cannibals but escaped just in time!"

"Well that's a good story. I hope your cannibals don't eat sheep now there aren't enough tourists for them for them to feast on!"

Things to think about

- Why were all the people they met (apart from the cannibals) so helpful? Think about how we get news of what is happening in our world and what Neria's people would use instead of TV and newspapers.

- What might have happened if Édouard hadn't managed to scare the cannibals away?

Chapter 16 Back home

I'd promised to explain to Neria about eclipses of the sun and I really did try but I needed to convince her about things she was certain were impossible.

I told her the sun was 93 million miles away and the moon only a quarter of a million miles: so they looked the same size even though the sun was much bigger. When it was a new moon, you couldn't see the moon because the sun shone on the far side of the moon. If the Earth and the moon and the sun were all in a line, the moon sometimes went in front of the sun and seemed to take a bite out of the sun or, very rarely, completely hide the sun for a few minutes.

That all made sense to me but if, like Neria, I thought the sun and the moon were gods and that the Earth was flat, not a ball bigger than the moon and smaller than the sun, I would have assumed that my story was no more than a fairy story which was just what Neria did.

That evening, when we were each in our own bed in my room, Neria said "I don't think I'll ever understand your world. I would need to be a magician like you to know how it works and how to make it do the things that I want. It's not like that for you when you visit my world: where there are lots of things you can't do or make happen, like electricity or cars that go on their own, but you can understand my world and learn how to hunt and cook and look after babies. I think you would be happy in my world but I can only ever be interested, not happy, in yours. Why don't you come home with me and live in my world for ever?"

It was a bit tempting despite the risk of cannibals. Everyone of Neria relatives thought I was a magician: I could become an important man and maybe Neria and I would want to marry one day. But there were loads of things I'd have to practise: I was hopeless at making flint tools and starting fires and hunting for example.

Although getting good at all these things would be interesting, I did wonder about whether living a life in a world that never changed would be boring. Neria's great grandparents to her great grandchildren would live in exactly the same world until, some thousands of years in her future, someone learned how to farm and then how to make metals. My world was completely different from the one my great grandparents lived in and my own grandchildren will probably be able to do things I have never even dreamed of. Of course my world might go horribly wrong – there is constant talk about global warming, extinctions, over-population and all sorts of other problems that may get really serious in my lifetime but I don't know when or how serious they will be. I might even be able to help solve some of the problems when I'm grown up. I already knew what Neria's world will be like for hundreds and thousands of years.

I suppose the real reason I made my decision was because I wanted to be with my parents and my friends in my world. But Neria was more than just a real friend: she had taught me lots and let me experience things that no one else in my world has seen. She had only lived in my world for a few days but I had been in her world for months over the summer – she had been my only friend and I loved her.

I asked Neria why we couldn't go on visiting each other and she said the problem was that her clan was going to move north because the herds of reindeer seemed to be moving north too. The cave tunnel was the only way we had to go to and from each other's worlds. "Won't you come back home sometimes? Then we could meet again and you can tell me all about life in the north lands." She thought that might work but she had no idea how long it would be before she got back home. "It doesn't really matter does it? When I come back it will be the same time that I left you, so you'll see me straight away if you wait a few minutes, even if I spend a long time in the north."

With that promise of a future meeting, one I hoped would be the first of many more, we agreed to split-up and each live in our own world with our own families.

The next day we climbed up to the hot springs, had a last swim together and then got dressed in the right clothes for our own worlds. She told me to keep my Goat God clothes she had made for me, just in case I visited her world again. I wanted to kiss her goodbye but she said "Don't be silly, just wait a few minutes after I've gone and I'll be back."

So we just held hands for a few moments and then waved each other goodbye.

I decided to get ready for another swim with Neria when she got back in a few minutes. I was just ready to start my swim when Neria reappeared from the cave, looking around her as though she had never been here before. She was accompanied by a lady I'd never seen before and who looked about the same age as my Mum. She called out "Can Alasme swim with you Édouard?" and I realised that the girl looked almost exactly like Neria but a bit different. And how did the lady know my name?

She soon started to explain. "So the cave passage still works even after all this time. I've been away in the north for almost twenty years. I couldn't get back before but I promised to visit you again when I could, so here I am. Alasme is my daughter and I've told her all about you and even taught her a bit of your language.

I ought to have been so pleased to have seen Neria again but I wasn't. I wanted the friend of my own age who had been my companion on all our adventures. Instead she was a grown-up with a daughter. She said she also had two small children at home who were being looked after by her sister for the short time she would be away.

Looking at Neria she seemed not just different, grown-up and a mother, but sad too: perhaps she was remembering our childhood together like I was.

I asked if she would be staying near the cave tunnel for long and she said no. Her home was in the far north now but Alasme was going to stay here with her aunt because she wanted to learn the best way of training the tame wolves they had bred from Kumia: the one we caught twenty years ago.

Neria said "Your parents still think I'm a lost child. We need to get that sorted out before I go back to the north in my world. Alasme, I want you to pretend to be called Neria for a little while. Édouard, let's go and meet your Mum and Dad.

As soon as they saw us, Mum called out "Hello you two" and Alasme had the good sense to join me in replying "Hello".

Neria immediately began thanking Mum and Dad for finding her daughter and looking after her so well. Mum and Dad had obviously worried quite a lot about having a lost child that even the police had failed to trace, so they were delighted when Neria's Mum turned up.

We all had a quick meal and Alasme remembered she was being Neria for the whole time. The real Neria explained how she got separated from her daughter while she was staying with friends and had only just tracked her down.

My Mum said Neria had been a delightful guest and friend for me and could come again whenever she liked. Alasme said "Can I Mum?" and Neria said "Thank you, I'm sure she will love to come but now we need to get home . Please can you tell everyone to stop looking for her?" I said I'd go with them so I knew where they lived.

At thc warm lake Alasme wanted the swim we hadn't had time for earlier. Neria said she wanted to get home and Alasme could follow after her swim.

Neria looked quite sad as she entered the cave and I thought she was crying but she turned away so I couldn't see for certain.

When we were dried and getting dressed, Alasme said "Mummy wanted me to show you these. She says they are one of her most treasured possessions."

She opened a little leather purse and tipped out a necklace of nine one-centime pieces. "There were ten but she gave one to Daddy when they had their first baby: that was me."

I asked Alasme if she would like to come swimming again tomorrow. "Yes please – I'll bring you a bit of meat to cook, can you bring your magic matches?"

Things to think about

- Do you think Neria wished she had chosen to stay in our world?
- What might happen to Alasme and Édouard over the next few years?

The names of all the people in Neria's world, and all her words in this book, are Basque words. Many people think that Basque is a very old language and similar to the language of the Stone Age. It would not have been exactly the same .

Look at this part of a story (called Sir Gawain and the Green Knight) written in English about 700 years ago – it is very difficult to understand. So Neria's language would have been very different from what today's Basque people speak.

Siþen þe ſege ⁊ þe aſſaut watȝ ſeſed at troye
þe borȝ brittened ⁊ brent to brondeȝ ⁊ aſkeȝ
þe tulk þat þe trāmes of treſoū þ' wroȝt
watȝ tried for his tricherie þe treweſt on erthe
hit watȝ Ennias þe athel ⁊ his high' kynde
þat ſiþen depreced p̄uinces ⁊ patroūes bicome
welneȝe of al þe wele ī þe weſt iles
fro riche romulus to rome ricchis hȳ ſwyþe
w[t] gret bobbaūce þat burȝe he biges vpon fyrſt
⁊ neuenes hit his aune nome as hit now hat
ticius to tuſkan ⁊ teldes bigȳnes
lang aberde ī lūbardie lyftes vp homes wyth wȳne
⁊ fer ou' þe french flod felix brut9
on mony bonkkes ful brode bretayn he ſetteȝ
where werre ⁊ wrake ⁊ wonder
bi ſyþeȝ hatȝ wont þ' īne

Poppy's Moth

Older children might like this book, It is intended for children of about 12 to 18 – the same ages as the two main characters.

It is available on Amazon as a kindle ebook or as a paperback book.

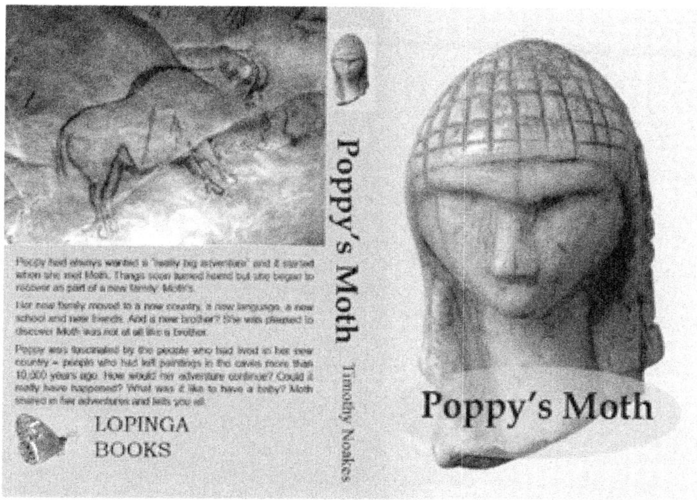

Poppy had always wanted a "really big adventure" and it started when she met Moth. Things soon turned horrid but she began to recover as part of a new family: Moth's.
Her new family moved to a new country, a new language, a new school and new friends. And a new brother? She was pleased to discover Moth was not at all like a brother.

Poppy was fascinated by the people who had lived in her new country – people who had left paintings in the caves more than 10,000 years ago. How would her adventure continue? Could it really have happened? What was it like to have a baby? Moth shared in her adventures and tells you all.

Printed in Great Britain
by Amazon

61686154R00068